JASON
AND THE GOLDEN
FLEECE

ARACHNE THE SPINNER

D1079379

For Ethel

JASON
AND THE
GOLDEN FLEECE

ARACHNE THE SPINNER

GERALDINE McCAUGHREAN

ILLUSTRATED BY TONY ROSS

ORCHARD BOOKS

ORCHARD BOOKS
96 Leonard Street, London EC2A 4RH
Orchard Books Australia
14 Mars Road, Lane Cove, NSW 2066
ISBN 1 86039 435 3 (hardback)
ISBN 1 86039 527 9 (paperback)
First published in Great Britain 1997
First paperback publication 1998
Text © Geraldine McCaughrean 1992
Illustrations © Tony Ross 1997
1 2 3 4 5 6 02 01 00 99 98
A CIP catalogue record for this book is available from the
British Library.
Printed in Great Britain

JASON AND THE GOLDEN FLEECE

It's sad, but sometimes brothers hate
each other. Pelias hated his older
brother, Aeson, because Aeson was the
King of Thebes. "I want to be king,"
said Pelias, and took the throne from
his brother and put him in prison.

But Aeson had a son, and after many years that son came back to fight for his father's rights. His name was Jason.

When Pelias heard that Jason had arrived, he did not send assassins to kill him. He challenged him to a dare. "I'll give up the crown without a fight, if

you can prove you are worthy to take it from me. I dare you to go and find the famous Golden Fleece. If you can bring it to me, the crown goes back to your father."

"I accept! I'll do it!" said Jason.

Then Pelias smiled a wicked smile. For he knew that many had tried to take the fiercely-guarded Golden Fleece belonging to King Aeëtes—but none had lived to tell the tale.

Jason's first task was to search out the finest shipbuilder in the land.

"Build me a ship finer than any that ever sailed the seas. I'm going in search of the Golden Fleece!"

"But they say the Fleece is guarded by a dragon that never sleeps!" whispered the shipbuilder.

"Then I must put that dragon to sleep for ever!" cried Jason.

He called his ship *Argo*, which means swift, and he mustered a crew from all

the heroes of the world and called them his Argonauts. But when he climbed aboard, he did not even know where to start looking for the Golden Fleece.

Resting his hand on the wooden figurehead—carved from a magical oak tree—he could feel a throb, like a heartbeat. Suddenly the figurehead turned, and the carved eyes opened, and the carved mouth spoke: "King Phineas will tell you where. Ask poor, poor Phineas!"

Phineas was old and blind. He had
chests full of robes and larders full of
food. But when Jason and the Argonauts

visited him he was
as thin as a twig
and his clothes
hung in rags.

Servants
brought delicious
food. But no
sooner was the
table set than in
through the
windows swooped
a flock of hideous
birds, their claws
snatching, their

wings clacking. They had women's heads, with flying hair and munching mouths, and they stole the supper out of the very hands of the Argonauts and slashed at their faces.

"The Harpies! Shelter under the

table, sirs!" cried King Phineas. "You'll be safer there."

But Jason drew his sword and cried, "Up, men, and fight!"

He and his crew fought the Harpies until feathers and hair fell like snow.

The creatures beat at Jason with their leathery wings, but he cut them out of the air with his sword and jumped on them with his two feet. At last the Harpies fled shrieking across the roof-tops and out to sea, never to return.

Jason filled a plate with food and set it in front of the king. "Eat, friend, then tell us how to find the Golden Fleece."

"Don't try it!" begged Phineas. "The Fleece hangs in the Land of Colchis, beyond the Clashing Cliffs. Think of that and tremble!"

"Tremble? I, tremble? Ha!" said Jason grandly. And he gathered his men together and the *Argo* set sail for the Clashing Cliffs.

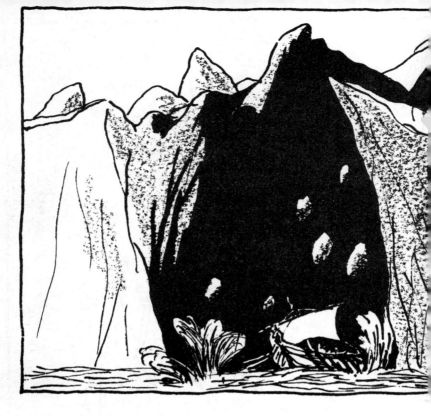

But the cliffs were a terrifying sight.
Two walls of rock, on either side of a
narrow strait, crashed together like
cymbals. Fire streamed down and
sparks flew up, while boulders plunged
into the churning sea below.

"We shall be ground to dust!" cried the Argonauts.

"No! Watch the seagulls, men!" cried Jason. "They know when the way ahead is safe. Lean on your oars, and follow the gulls!"

And between one clash of cliffs and the next, the *Argo* sped through, swift as the darting seagulls. Soon they had reached Colchis, Land of the Golden Fleece.

The next day Jason presented himself to the king of the island and told him his

story. "I must have the Golden Fleece—it's my destiny," he said.

The king's lip curled. "Well, of course I shall let you take my Golden Fleece ... but the soldiers who guard it might try to stop you. Ha ha!"

Out of his deep purple pockets he pulled handfuls of sharp white teeth.

Dragon's teeth! He tossed them in
among the Argonauts. As each tooth
touched the ground, a warrior sprang
up, bristling with weapons. Soon these

soldiers outnumbered Jason's men a hundred to one.

"We fought the Harpies, didn't we?" cried Jason to his men. "Surely we can

knock out a
mouthful of
teeth!"

"Kill them!"
the king raged at
his dragon-tooth
army. But soon
there was no army
left to hear him.
The Argonauts
had wiped it out. Now nothing stood
between Jason and the Golden Fleece.

Except the dragon.

The Fleece hung in a lovely garden. By
the gate of the garden stood a woman
— the king's daughter. "I watched you

fight the dragon-tooth warriors," said
Princess Medea to Jason. "You are a
true hero, I can see that. But you'll
need my magic if you are going to win
the Golden Fleece. Marry me and I'll
help you."

"You're so beautiful that I'll
willingly marry you," said Jason. "But I

must lift down the prize by my own strength or I would be cheating."

He set out through flowery groves, across streams, past bushes hung with blossom. But here and there he passed piles of bones. Other heroes had entered the garden before him ... and met the dragon.

At last Jason found the prize he had come for. The Golden Fleece rested over the branch of a tree—as thick and heavy as a carpet, glistening with golden curls, soft, soft, soft. And round the tree coiled the dragon set to guard it. The monster had no eyelids, it had no name and it had no pity. It looked at Jason with eyes scorched red by sunshine and moonlight. Then it pounced on him with gaping jaws.

Jason drew his sword, but its blade shattered like glass against the dragon's scales. Teeth tore his clothes and fiery breath scorched his hair. Up into the tree he clambered to escape. And when the dragon opened its mouth to lick

him down, Jason plunged in his broken
sword. The beast gave a terrible roar.
Smoke billowed round Jason. Again
and again he stabbed, until black
smoke dirtied all the king's garden.

The Argonauts, watching from the
shore, saw the smoke gather in the sky.

"Where's Jason? Why doesn't he come?" they cried.

Then the sun glinted on a splash of gold—a sheep's fleece. It was draped over Jason's shoulder as he came running down the beach. Alongside him ran a woman as beautiful as the Fleece.

"Aboard, men!" cried Jason. "I've stolen the king's Golden Fleece and his daughter!"

So Jason and Princess Medea returned to Thebes—much to the amazement and fury of Pelias. Jason's father, Aeson,

was freed from prison, but he refused
to put on the crown of Thebes again.

"I'm too tired to rule, Son," he said.
"You must be king in my place."

But Medea said gently, "Trust me,
father-in-law. I have magic to make you
strong and young again."

She poured him a peculiar potion,
which sent Aeson to sleep for three days.

When he awoke, he had the body of a young man and the wisdom of an old one—and all the energy he needed to rule Thebes.

When wicked old Pelias saw this amazing transformation, he went to Medea and offered her all his money if she would do the same for him. "Make me young again, Medea," he said. "I'd give anything for that!"

So Medea gave him a potion, too, and he fell asleep for three days. Three months. Three years. In fact he never woke up again, because Medea had put him to sleep for ever.

So Jason and Medea lived together as man and wife, and although Jason dressed in simple clothes, his cloak was lined with a golden fleece.

ARACHNE THE SPINNER

Once, when all cloths and clothes were woven by hand, there was a needle-woman called Arachne more skilful than all the rest. Her tapestries were so lovely that people paid a fortune to buy them. Tailors and weavers came from miles around just to watch Arachne at work on her loom. Her shuttle flew to and fro, and her fingers plucked the

strands as if she were making music rather than cloth.

"The gods certainly gave you an amazing talent," said her friends.

"Gods? Bodkins! There's nothing the gods could teach me about weaving. I can weave better than any god or goddess."

Her friends turned rather pale. "Better not let the goddess Athene hear you say that."

"Don't care who hears it. I'm the best there is," said Arachne.

An old lady sitting behind her examined the yarns Arachne had spun that morning, feeling their delightful texture between finger and thumb. "So if there were a competition between you and the goddess Athene, you think you would win?" she said.

"She wouldn't stand a chance," said Arachne. "Not against me."

All of a sudden the old lady's grey hair began to float like smoke about her head and turn to golden light.

A swish of wind blew her old coat into
shreds and revealed
a breastplate of
silver and a robe
of dazzling
white. She grew
taller and taller
until she stood
head and
shoulders
above the
crowd. There
was no
mistaking the
beautiful
grey-eyed
goddess, Athene.

"Let it be so!" declared Athene.
"A contest between you and me."

Arachne's friends fell on their faces in awe. But Arachne simply threaded another shuttle. And although her face was rather pale and her hands did tremble a little, she smiled and said, "A contest then. To see who is the best needlewoman in the world."

To and fro went the shuttles, faster than birds building a nest.

Athene wove a picture of Mount Olympus. All the gods were there: heroic, handsome, generous, clever and kind. She wove all the creatures of creation on to her loom. And when she wove a kitten, the crowd sighed,

"Aaaah!" When she wove a horse, they wanted to reach out and stroke it.

Alongside her sat Arachne, also weaving a picture of the gods.

But it was a comical picture. It showed all the silly things the gods had ever done: dressing up, squabbling, lazing about and bragging. In fact she made them look just as foolish as ordinary folk.

But oh! when she pictured a butterfly sitting on a blade of grass, it looked as if it would fly away at any moment. When she wove a lion, the crowd shrieked and ran away in fright. Her sea shimmered and her corn waved, and her finished tapestry was more beautiful than nature itself.

Athene laid down her shuttle and came to look at Arachne's weaving. The crowd held its breath.

"You are the better weaver," said the goddess. "Your skill is matchless. Even I don't have your magic."

Arachne preened herself and grinned with smug satisfaction. "Didn't I tell you as much?"

"But your pride is even greater than your skill," said Athene. "And your cheekiness is past all forgiving." She pointed at Arachne's tapestry. "Make fun of the gods, would you? Well, for that I'll make such an example of you that no one will ever make the same mistake again!"

She took the shuttle out of Arachne's hands and pushed it into her mouth. Then, just as Athene had changed from an old woman into her true shape, she transformed Arachne.

The girl's arms stuck to her sides, and left only her long, clever fingers straining and scrabbling. Her body shrank down to a black blob no bigger

than an ink blot: an end of thread still
curled out of its mouth. Athene used
the thread to hang Arachne up on a
tree, and left her dangling there.

"Weave your tapestries for ever!"
said the goddess. "And however
wonderful they are, people will only

shudder at the sight of them and pull them to shreds."

It all came true. For Arachne had been turned into the first spider, doomed for ever to spin webs in the corners of rooms, in bushes, in dark, unswept places. And though cobwebs are as lovely a piece of weaving as you'll ever see, just look how people hurry to sweep them away.

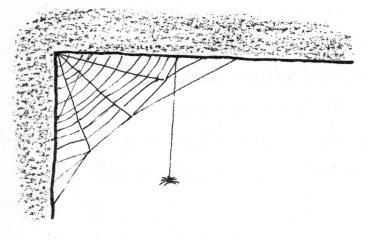